As always, to Henry: taller, smarter and braver
than his old mum, but my baby nonetheless! A.S.

To Jack & Bertie xx G.B.

First published in Great Britain in 2017 by Andersen Press Ltd.,

20 Vauxhall Bridge Road, London SW1V 2SA.

Text copyright © Anthea Simmons, 2017.

Illustration copyright © Georgie Birkett, 2017.

The rights of Anthea Simmons and Georgie Birkett

to be identified as the author and illustrator

of this work have been asserted by them in accordance with the

Copyright, Designs and Patents Act, 1988.

Printed and bound in China.

1   3   5   7   9   10   8   6   4   2

British Library Cataloguing in Publication Data available.

ISBN 978 1 78344 485 4

This book has been printed on acid-free paper

# I'm BIG Now!

Anthea Simmons    Georgie Birkett

ANDERSEN PRESS

There's a new baby now, I'm not the baby any more.

My little brother does the things I used to do before.

But sometimes I still want to be a baby, just the same,
so I found something new to play...

the baby big girl game!

Here's my special baby bed,
my brother sleeps there now.
I can still squeeze into it.
Let me show you how.

Mummy smiles and lifts me out
then sets me on the floor.

"You're my big girl, darling,
not a baby any more!"

These were my favourite baby clothes.
I want to try them on.

But they are
really tiny now.
My legs are
far too long.

Daddy smiles and teases me, "You're way too tall for those."

"Let's get you dressed and ready in your lovely big girl clothes."

The baby's got his mushy
food, he gets it in his hair.
But I've got crunchy cereal
and I sit on a chair.

"Would you like breakfast all mashed up?" Mummy teases me. "No!" I can eat my big girl food with big girl teeth, you see.

The baby's on the changing mat and he's not very happy.

I'm up on my potty. I don't have to wear a nappy.

"This was you,
once," Daddy
says. "You hated
nappies, too."

"I'm a big girl, now," I say. "I do what big girls do."

Baby plays with my old things,
my building blocks and toys,
and when I try to take them back
he makes a screechy noise.

Granny smiles and
hugs me tight and
gently strokes my hair.

"There's my clever grown-up girl,
learning how to share."

I've got a lovely car seat
that lets me sit up high.

Baby's in my old one,
being strapped in makes him cry.

"Don't worry little brother, it will not be for long." I make the trip go faster by singing him a song.

Baby's in my buggy and I'm running around.
I'm splashing in my wellies through the
puddles on the ground.

I don't need to ride home – I can skip and run – because I'm not a baby now, I'm big and having fun!

Joanne and
I play babies,
we crawl around
the floor.

We scream and
laugh and roll
about and then we
scream some more.

And if my brother looks upset,
we cuddle him and say,
"We're not babies any more
and you'll be big one day!"

The baby loves his bathtime,
now he comes in with me.
We make waves and splashes
and pretend we're in the sea.

Mummy wraps us up in towels
and hugs us very tight.

"My big girl and my baby boy. What a lovely sight!"

The baby's in his cot now
and I creep in to look.
He's got his fluffy teddy bear
and I've got my best book.

It's nice to be a baby
but sometimes
boring, too!

It's much more fun
to do the things
that all us big girls do.

Now I'm very sleepy after
all that fun and play,
I've had my bedtime story
– the best end to my day.

My parents whisper in my ear,
"Night, night, our little star!"